THE GUUD BOOK

ABOUT INFERTILITY

by
Camille T.C.Hammond MD, MPH

Illustrated by Ana Patankar

The GUUD Book
About Infertility

Copyright © 2017 Dr.Camille Hammond

Cover Design and Illustration by: Ana Patankar

Book Illustrations by: Ana Patankar

Book Layout and Design: Ana Patankar

www.guudbooks.com

Forward

GUUD (urban dictionary): Someone or something who or which is truly, in all aspects of the word, "Good".

Dedication

This book is dedicated to my savior, Jesus Christ, for giving me a voice and a story to share. It is also dedicated to my family (Jason, Aaron, Kai, Simone, Ron and Tinina, Pam, Gary, Simone, Alexis, Ron and so many others), friends who listened and then acted with courage, and to everyone on the family building journey. Finally it is dedicated to the staff, Trustees and Advisory council members, families and supporters of the Tinina Q. Cade Foundation and to all of the soldiers (doctors, nurses, embryologists, adoption coordinators, administrators etc.) who tirelessly serve families OVERCOMING infertility. Thank you all for your GUUD work.

Terri and Jaq were a very happy couple.
They liked going out to the movies, making corny private
jokes at which only they laughed, and playing footsie under
the table at dinner. They were just like
all couples who are deeply in love.

Terri loved Jaq's eyes and Jaq thought Terri had the best hairline and chin she'd ever seen. They were very much *in love* and loved, loved, loved spending time together. They liked each other as well. They had long deep conversations about things like gas prices, the flavor of coffee and their mutual appreciation of sand between their toes.

2

Terri and Jaq woke up one morning and
decided they were ready to start their family.
They looked at each other and both spoke at the same time
(even before they had a chance to brush their teeth)!
"Let's Have A Baby!"
Jaq then squealed
"It can be our project!"

So they started working on the "having a baby project" immediately. They *worked* on this every morning and every night. At first it was a lot of fun and it felt more like they were playing more than *working*. The playing was GUUD.

4

But after a while – the playing started to feel more like work. It stopped being so fun. Terri told his best friend Taj that he and Jaq had been trying to 'make a baby' for 8 months, but that they hadn't gotten pregnant.

Taj sat down and thought about this for a minute. Then she looked across the table at Terri and asked, "Have you relaxed yet?" Terri replied, "It's kinda hard to relax when you're stressed out. This 'making a baby stuff' is stressful!"

6

That night- Taj went online and looked up lots of info about getting pregnant for Terri and Jaq. Then she asked her co-workers and family members for advice about getting pregnant. The next day she typed everything up in her favorite font - BRAGGADOCIO, saved it in the color emerald green and printed out the 17 pages of advice she had gathered for her friends.

Terri smiled and thanked Taj and followed Jaq out to the car. As soon as they closed the car door, Jaq's eyes began to well with tears. She was sad-and mad-and confused. They had tried some of the things Taj suggested but not everything. She rolled her eyes and mumbled more to herself than to Terri. "Taj isn't even trying to get pregnant so how did she know all of this stuff? Also, some of the advice was 'totally garbage.' Standing on your head after *working* for 5 minutes? Who can do that? Most yogis can't even do that. That's dumb. But maybe I can try...."

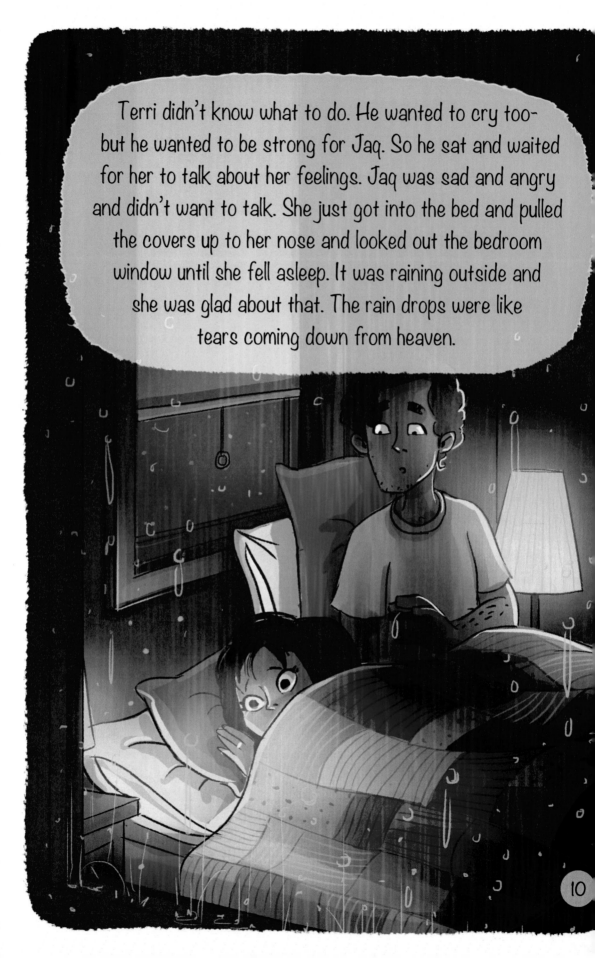

Terri didn't know what to do. He wanted to cry too— but he wanted to be strong for Jaq. So he sat and waited for her to talk about her feelings. Jaq was sad and angry and didn't want to talk. She just got into the bed and pulled the covers up to her nose and looked out the bedroom window until she fell asleep. It was raining outside and she was glad about that. The rain drops were like tears coming down from heaven.

After sulking for a few days (with no *working*)
Terri decided it was time to talk to a doctor about their
"project." Taj had mentioned a website that had information
on all of the fertility clinics in the US that day in the coffee
shop. That was one thing Terri actually remembered.
He visited the site to learn about local fertility clinics
(http://www.sart.org/Find_A_Clinic/). Then he shared
all of the information with Jaq and together they picked a
fertility clinic. Then together they called the clinic
to set up an appointment.

No appointment was available for 3 months...
so, they spent their time avoiding baby showers, learning about local support groups and shopping at odd hours in hopes that they would not bump into pregnant women or people with small children.

While they waited they also dealt with having to decide whether to go to the family cookout because of all of the young children in the family and the aunties and uncles who would surely ask them, "When are you two going to have babies?"

While waiting they also charted Jaq's basal body temperature (put the thermometer in your mouth as soon as you wake up, before your feet hit the floor; when it increases by a degree or so you are ovulating- time to immediately *work* - do not stop, do not pass go, everything must cease until you have *worked*... Get busy)!

They alternated between avoiding the internet and reading everything they could find about infertility online, then avoiding the internet again.

And they took lots of pregnancy tests and noticed every single change in Jaq's body function - (her pee was a little more orange than usual today - take a pregnancy test; her period is 12 minutes late this month - take a test; she's feeling a bit nauseous after eating a huge meal - take a test; she's gaining weight - take a test)...

Praying... A LOT!

And more *working*....

Then FINALLY the day came for them to visit their fertility doctor. This was over a year after they started *working* to have a baby.

They got up, put on clothes that were nice, but not too nice. Jaq thought "got to seem like this is casual and like it's no big deal, but it is a really, really big deal... but you know..."

Terri agreed.

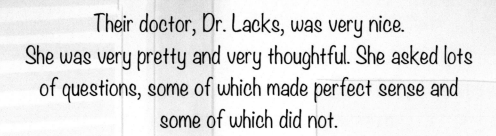

Their doctor, Dr. Lacks, was very nice.
She was very pretty and very thoughtful. She asked lots
of questions, some of which made perfect sense and
some of which did not.

"How long have you been off birth control? Have you ever
gotten pregnant in the past? What is your goal- to become
pregnant and/or to become a parent? Are you taking any
vitamins? Do you exercise? Do you smoke? Has anyone
in your family ever struggled with infertility?"
On and on she asked...

Dr. Lacks shared that ⅓ of the infertility cases were caused by male issues, ⅓ were caused by female issues and ⅓ was caused by unknown issues. She said that there were many, many types of treatments available.
These included some of the following:

IVF

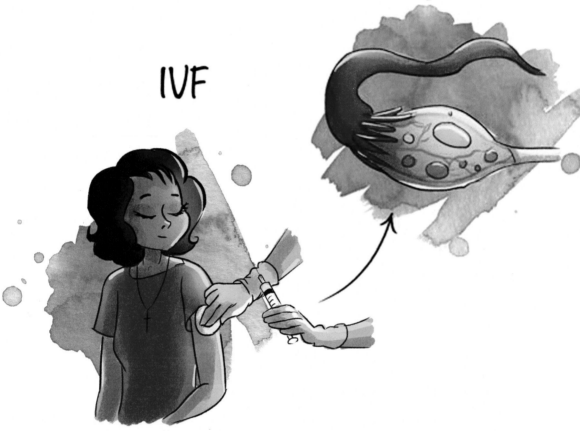

The mom-to-be takes meds to mature more than one egg. When her ovaries get large with mature eggs the doctor removes them by inserting a large needle from the vagina into the ovary. Separately, the dad-to-be goes into a "special" room with lots of magazines and a television with lots of adult movies and comes out with a container full of sperm.

The embryologist takes her eggs, adds his sperm and
fertilization takes place and the resulting embryos are monitored
over the next 5 days or so until 1 or 2 (usually just one) is
transferred back into the womb. Transfer is on day 3 when the
embryo is at the 6-8 cell stage or on day 5 which is the
blastocyst stage. (Cost $12-15,000)

IVF with ICSI

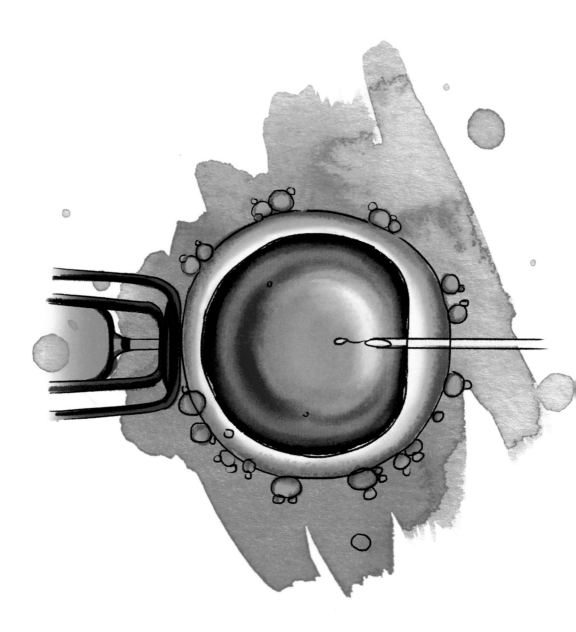

This is IVF but instead of fertilization taking place
the usual way, an embryologist selects one sperm that is normal
and injects it into the egg.
(IVF cost +$1500 - $2000)

Donor egg

This is the same as the IVF option except the egg comes
from a different person.
(IVF cost PLUS another $5000-50,000)

Donor sperm

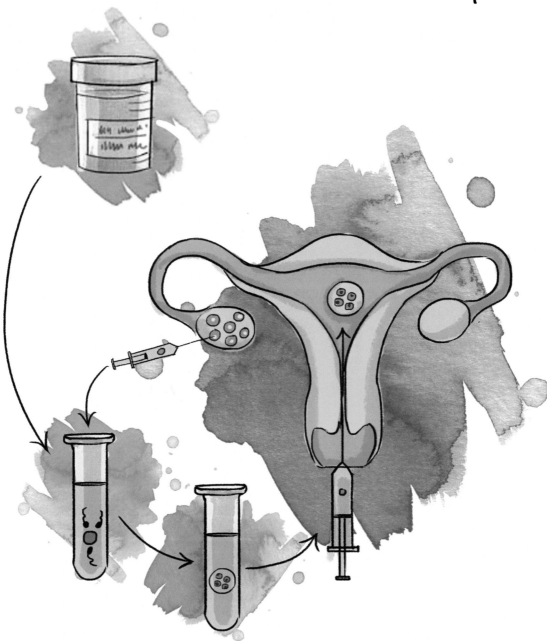

This can involve IVF if there are female issues.
Otherwise sperm is purchased and inserted into the cervix
at the right time.
($500 to $5000)

Gestational Carrier

This is also referred to as a surrogate, but a surrogate is someone who uses her own eggs and carries a baby for an intended family. A Gestational Carrier receives eggs from the intended mother, or a donor, and sperm from the intended father, or a donor, and carries the embryo and delivers the baby.
(IVF PLUS free to $100,000)

And, just in case they had not already considered it, adopting a baby was a great option as well. This could include...

Private adoption

This is usually through a private agency that worked with birth mothers. Birth mothers would read applications of the families that fit their criteria and select a family that they want to raise their child/children. A couple is more likely to receive a newborn baby with this option. It can cost different amounts based on the agency.
($10-50k)

Public adoption

This is adoption from the foster care system.
The children are usually older and this process requires
families become certified as foster care families first.
(Usually free)

Then Dr. Lacks ordered tests for both Terri and Jaq. Jaq had to have a blood test and the results showed her estrogen level, progesterone, AMH (Anti-Mullerian Hormone), and FSH. The amount of FSH in a woman's blood guts up when she ovulates. She also looked at Jaq's ovaries using an ultrasound and her fallopian tubes using a hysterosalpingogram.

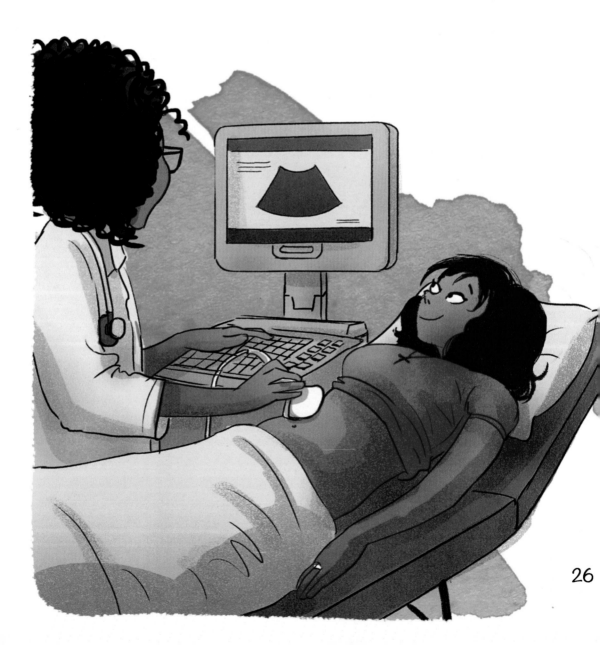

Terri went into the "special room" with movies and magazines and came out with a sperm sample. This sample was tested for:

1) The amount of liquid it contained.
2) The shape of the sperm (did they have 1 head or 2 heads).
3) The direction the sperm swam.
4) The number of sperm in the sample.

After all the testing was complete the doctor recommended that Terri and Jaq have IVF (in vitro fertilization). The cost was going to be $12,500 for one cycle and another $5000 for the medicine. Terri and Jaq had insurance and lived in Maryland, so thankfully they had some medical insurance coverage, but they still needed to pay $3500 out of pocket for co-pays and costs that were not covered by their insurance.

Terri and Jaq looked at each other and exclaimed "What are we going to do? Where will we get the money?"

There are lots of organizations that have grants for families with infertility. Some require that you live in a certain area and some only fund families that don't already have kids. Some also are only for patients at specific clinics. Most require a diagnosis of infertility. The Tinina Q Cade Foundation is one of the few programs that offers grants to help infertile families with adoption and fertility treatment costs.

Other ways to raise the money include getting a part-time job, selling stuff on E-bay, asking friends and family members for financial support, cutting expenses, using savings and retirement funds and volunteering for medical research studies.

Terri and Jaq decided that they might apply for a grant if they did not get pregnant with the first cycle of IVF. They both chose to take part time jobs driving with a ridesharing company to raise the money to begin their first cycle of IVF. Once they raised the $3500, they began.

Every day, while they were going through the first IVF cycle, they sat next to the same couple at the fertility clinic. The room was full of people but no one looked at each other and everyone tried to avoid bumping into or touching each other.

Then one day, Jaq smiled at the woman sitting next to her and they started to talk about how weird it was sitting in a full room where everyone was pretending not to see one another. Every day following that one they talked to each other in the waiting room. They became "fertility friends" while sitting at the clinic, waiting every morning for blood work and monitoring. The blood work involved getting blood drawn every day to test for hormones. The monitoring involved having a pelvic ultrasound every day to look at the size of the ovaries.

Their fertility friends became like family to Jaq and Terri. They followed each other on social media and did things like go out to the movies and make corny inside jokes. They even hosted "Friendsgiving," and ate turkey and drank pumpkin spiced cider together.

Terri and Jaq also started to attend a support group for help handling infertility. And, with new friends who understood their journey, Terri and Jaq started to feel less alone and more relaxed.

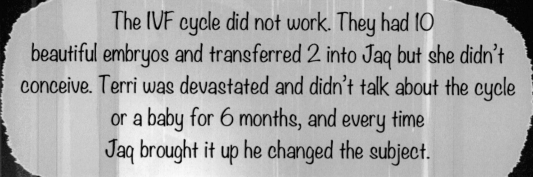

The IVF cycle did not work. They had 10 beautiful embryos and transferred 2 into Jaq but she didn't conceive. Terri was devastated and didn't talk about the cycle or a baby for 6 months, and every time Jaq brought it up he changed the subject.

About the IVF…

Let's have one more coffee!

34

Terri was angry, hurt, disappointed, relieved, and just wanted his old Jaq back. Just before the results came back, *working* was getting to be fun again because they weren't *trying* to get pregnant. They were just playing and finding each other like they used to do.

Jaq was angry that her fertility friend did conceive during that cycle. She felt betrayed by her own body and by the friend for getting pregnant and leaving her behind. But her fertility friend didn't give up on Jaq. She forgave her for being rude and for not returning calls.

After a little while, Jaq thought that even though her fertility friend was pregnant, she was still nice and funny. And, she didn't post every single symptom of her pregnancy on social media or share a photo of her pregnant belly every day. So Jaq decided that they could still be friends.

So they prayed about their future, they planned and they *worked*. It was GUUD and they moved forward with one of the options the doctor had shared months before.

Terri and Jaq continued to *work* and to listen to one another and believed that it was still possible for them to become parents. They never gave up even though it was hard and they needed to take a break from trying to conceive. In time, Jaq was ready to begin again and they tried something different. And that didn't work! When one of them got overwhelmed they stopped and just *worked* for fun and reconnected.

42

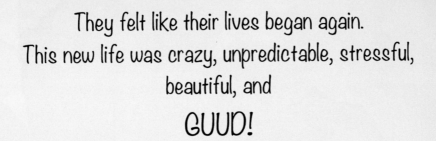

They felt like their lives began again.
This new life was crazy, unpredictable, stressful,
beautiful, and

GUUD!

Proceeds from this novel and all GUUD Books on Tough Topics will support the Tinina Q. Cade Foundation (Cade Foundation). The Cade Foundation is a non-profit that was started in 2005 to help needy families OVERCOME infertility. The foundation was named after Dr Tinina Cade, mother of Dr Camille Hammond, CEO and co-founder of the Tinina Q. Cade Foundation. Camille and her husband, Dr Jason Hammond, started the foundation as a resource for families when they overcame infertility. Dr Cade served as their gestational carrier following 5 years of infertility and delivered the couples triplets at 55 years old. The Tinina Q. Cade Foundation provides education, support and grants for adoption and fertility treatment to families with infertility.

For more information
please visit www.cadefoundation.org

Made in the USA
Middletown, DE
30 September 2017